Text copyright © 2021 Alice Trinh
Illustrations copyright © 2021 Jade Le

All rights reserved. This book or any portion thereof
may not be reproduced or used in any manner whatsoever
without the express written permission of the publisher
except for the use of brief quotations in a book review.

Printed in USA

First edition 2021

ISBN: 978-1-7377126-0-2 (Hardcover)
ISBN: 978-1-7377126-1-9 (Paperback)
ISBN: 978-1-7377126-2-6 (Dust jacket)

Book cover design and illustrations by Jade Le

Dedicated

**To my Luna who inspires me
to be my best self.**

Tết, the Vietnamese New Year, is a big celebration filled with days of fun festivities. It is a special time for families to gather and celebrate together.

Let's check the Lunar calendar to see when **Tết** is coming! In Vietnam, everyone turns a year older on **Tết**. It is everyone's birthday!

There are **12 Vietnamese Zodiac animals.** Each animal represents one year and has different human personalities and traits. Which animal will this New Year be?

There is much to do to prepare for the *Tết* celebration…

First, we clean the house. There is no cleaning during **Tết** because we don't want to sweep out any good luck.

We make sure all our debts are paid to not have any bad feelings for the New Year.

We hang many decorations for *Tết*. The colors red and yellow symbolize good luck and happiness.

Beautiful lanterns, lights, and banners with parallel sentences (*câu đối*) are hung around the house.

Statues of the Gods of the Three Stars (*Phúc Lộc Thọ*) are displayed to bring happiness, prosperity, and good health to everyone in the home.

We decorate the altars for our ancestors with fruits, coins, and flowers.

Our ancestors visit us on **Tết** and bring more luck and prosperity to the family.

It is time for us to go to the flower market to buy **Tết** trees. The more flowers on a tree mean more luck for a family!

There are many lucky plants and flowers to choose from like peach blossoms (*hoa đào*), yellow apricot blossoms (*hoa mai*), and kumquat trees (*cây quất*).

Our families spend days together preparing food. Special **Tết** food includes sticky rice cakes (***bánh chưng***), Vietnamese sausage (***giò chả***), boiled chicken (***gà luộc***), and candied fruits (***mứt***).

Food is one of the best parts of **Tết**. In Vietnam, **Tết** is not just celebrated but literally eaten (***ăn Tết*** = eating the New Year).

Lastly, we lay out our new *Tết* clothing. Children wear traditional Vietnamese outfits called *áo dài*. Finally, the preparations are complete. *Tết* is here and it is time to bring in the New Year!

The Vietnamese tradition of *xông nhà* (the first guest to visit a home) is important. A person of good temper, morals, and success is lucky and can bring a year full of blessings to the host family.

The *Tết* celebration lasts for at least 3 days. The first day is for visiting family and relatives to show respect and gratitude.

The second day is for visiting friends.

The third day is for visiting teachers and coworkers. It is also a day for visiting the graves of our relatives.

Everyone wishes each other a Happy New Year (*Chúc Mừng Năm Mới*)!

Children wish their elders a long life of 100 years (*sống lâu trăm tuổi*)!

Lucky money *(lì xì)* is given to children to wish them good health, to do well in school, and to have good fortune.

At the family altars, incense sticks are lit to honor and remember the ancestors.

Smiles and laughter are abundant everywhere! The crackling of firecrackers can be heard all through the streets.
The beating of drums gives heart to lion dances in parades and festivals.

And of course, there are lots of delicious food for family and friends to share.

Tết is a tradition that celebrates family of the past, current, and future.

As we celebrate *Tết* traditions, we count our good fortune and are grateful for this special time when we can all gather together.

Made in United States
Troutdale, OR
01/22/2025

This book belongs to:

A Production of
FoxtaleBooks Publishing

Marvin Kirchner
Plutone Artstation

Kirchheimer Str.81
73265 Dettingen u.Teck
Germany

Illustrations &
Artistic Design
Marvin Kirchner

Text & Production
Marvin Kirchner
Carolin Kirchner

Translation & Editing
Carolin Kirchner

1st Edition 2023
© 2023 Plutone Artstation
© 2023 Foxtale Books

ISBN Paperback: **9798879458954**
Text © 2023 Marvin Kirchner

For more information,
visit **www.foxtale-books.com**

For our brave little heroine E.,
who took the big step of giving up
her pacifier.
With love, C. & M.

FREDDIE
MUST SAY GOODBYE TO HIS PACIFIER

Marvin Kirchner I Carolin Kirchner

Effortlessly Say Goodbye to the Pacifier.
It Can Be That Easy!

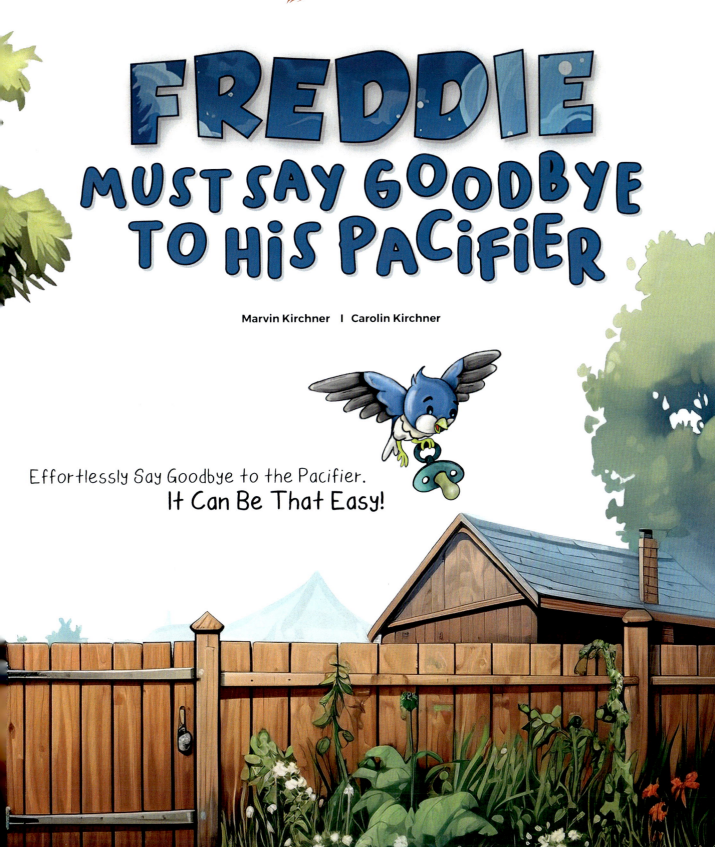

Once upon a time, there was a little bear named Freddie, whose best friend was a little pacifier. From the very beginning, he was a very calm and content bear. Even as a little baby, Freddie had his pacifier in his mouth. It went with him everywhere and made sure that Freddie felt safe and secure.

... while playing in the garden,

... in his room,

... while riding in the car,

... and of course, while sleeping.

One night, he had a special dream. He found himself in a forest full of pacifiers and he couldn't get enough of all the different shapes and colours. He walked through the forest and collected as many pacifiers as he could carry.

It was a wondrous place and Freddie was very happy...

The next morning, Freddie told his mama about his dream. "I dreamed about a forest full of binkies," he said excitedly. "It was so nice!"

But then Freddie's mama said something to him that Freddie hadn't expected:

"Freddie, my darling, it's time to say 'goodbye' to your pacifier. Look, at home and in the bear kindergarten, you don't need it anymore. You are now a big, brave bear. **It's time to fall asleep without your pacifier."**

Mama Bear added: "You know, the pacifier is not good for your little bear teeth either. And we want you to be healthy and strong, my little Freddie."

Freddie was worried about how he should fall asleep without his binky. He sighed. "But how will I manage that?"

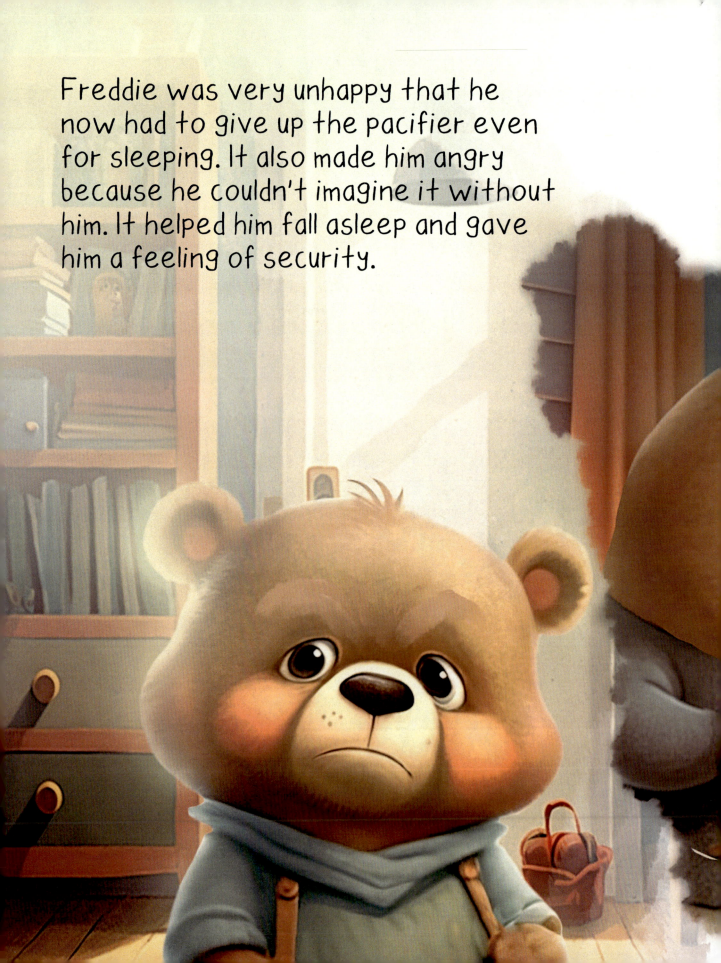

Freddie was very unhappy that he now had to give up the pacifier even for sleeping. It also made him angry because he couldn't imagine it without him. It helped him fall asleep and gave him a feeling of security.

Mama Bear compassionately told him that it was perfectly normal to be mad and angry when you have to part with something that means so much to you.
She stood by Freddie and encouraged him to overcome this challenge.

GRRRRR!!!

Luckily, Freddie's Papa had a **brilliant idea**. He gave Freddie a little box to paint, in which he could place his pacifier.

With the hearty support of Mama and Papa Bear, Freddie created a charming pacifier box, colourfully painted...

...and adorned with lots of love.

Freddie felt courage and bravery welling up inside him. That evening, he carefully placed his beloved pacifier into the box. His little bear heartbeat uncertainly, but Mama Bear was by his side. She smiled at him and snuggled with him into his soft bear bed.

Freddie's Pacifier Box

That night, Freddie fell fast asleep without his pacifier...

... He dreamed of an **enchanted forest** that was so mysterious and magical, Freddie felt like a brave explorer, ready to discover everything. It was an exciting adventure that Freddie would remember for a long time.

hu-hu-hu

When the first sunbeams tickled Freddie's face the next morning, he woke up feeling lively. Now it was time to get ready for bear kindergarten. And the pacifier box? It had completely slipped his mind in the excitement of the morning.

Little Freddie spent an exciting day at kindergarten. While playing and laughing with his friends, he forgot everything around him.

Freddie the Pirate!

When it was time to go home, he felt happy and secure, and that was all without his pacifier.

"Mama," he said proudly. "I think I can manage to fall asleep without a pacifier."

"I'm so happy to hear that, my dear," said his mama and gave him a kiss on the cheek. "You are so brave and strong."

"But what are we going to do with the pacifier box now?" Freddie asked curiously..

"That's for you to decide," Mama Bear answered with a smile.

Freddie thought for a moment. "I want **to bury the box in the garden.** That way, I can always remember how big I've become and how I gave up my pacifier."

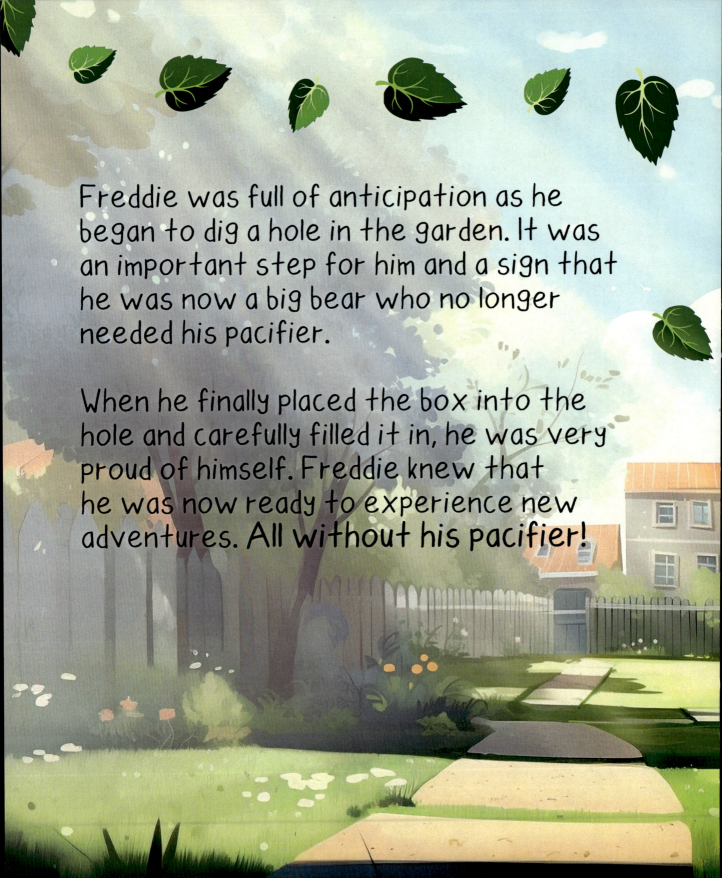

Freddie was full of anticipation as he began to dig a hole in the garden. It was an important step for him and a sign that he was now a big bear who no longer needed his pacifier.

When he finally placed the box into the hole and carefully filled it in, he was very proud of himself. Freddie knew that he was now ready to experience new adventures. All without his pacifier!

Freddie lit up at the thought. Together with Mama Bear, he carefully packed all his remaining pacifiers into a colourful little parcel. In big letters, they wrote: "Bear Baby Hospital". Freddie was happy that other little bears would now also enjoy his pacifiers.

"....and then I buried my very favourite pacifier in the garden, as a memory. The other pacifiers are now on their way to the little bear babies who can use them."

Full of pride, he told all the other bears in kindergarten about his adventure and *inspired them to also say goodbye to their pacifiers.*

That evening, Freddie fell asleep peacefully. He had completely forgotten about his pacifier.

Sleep well, little Freddie, and may your dreams be as sweet as a...

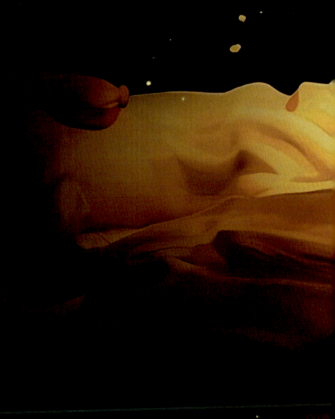

Dear Parents,

You've read the story, and your child is now ready to say goodbye to their pacifier? Fantastic. Then you can create a pacifier box together. Let your creativity run free and choose a small cardboard box or an old lunch box that your child can paint and decorate. Prepare them to place the pacifier into the box before going to bed. The box can be placed in the child's room, the bedroom, or another place.

It's essential that you sensitize your child to the weaning process and explain the importance of saying goodbye to a beloved habit. The book and the homemade pacifier box can help your child take this important step and look forward to a new phase in their life.

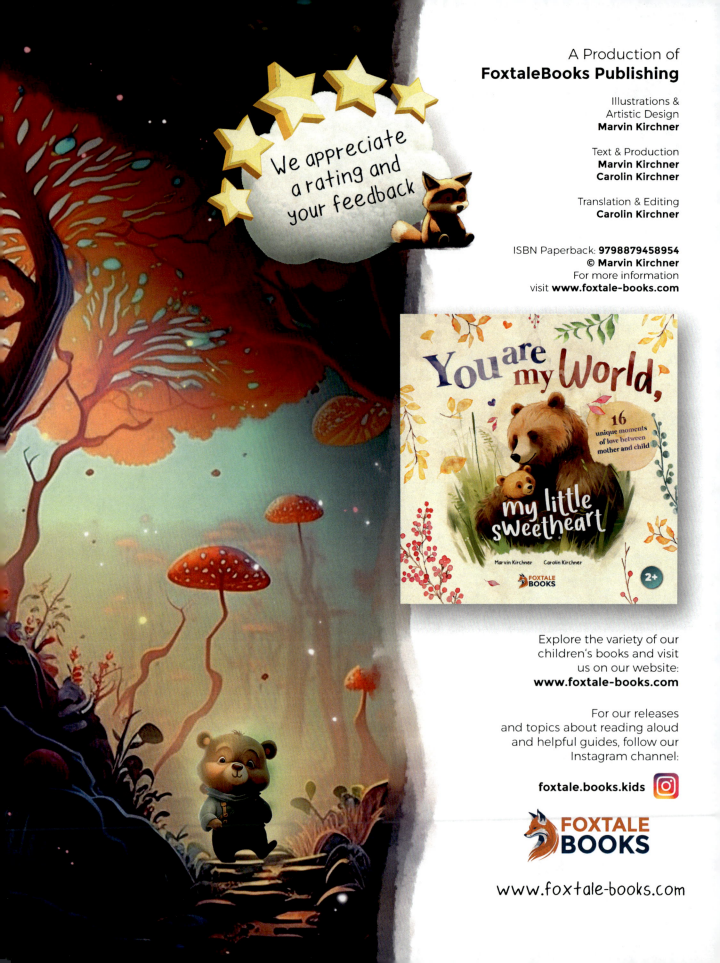